There are shoes to buckle, shoes to tie,

1

shoes too low,

and shoes too high.

Shoes to run in, shoes for sliding,

high-topped shoes for horseback riding.

Shoes too loose, shoes too tight,

shoes to snuggle in at night.

Shoes to skate in, shoes to skip in,

shoes to turn a double flip in.

Shoes for fishing, shoes for wishing,

rubber shoes for muddy squishing.

Shoes with ribbons, shoes with bows,

shoes to skate in when it snows.

Shoes for winter, shoes for fall,

shoes for spring, but best of all…

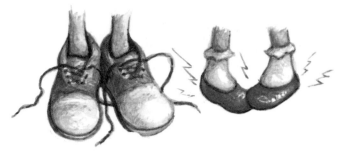

They're not too loose and not too tight.

They can be worn both day and night.

They're right for chasing, right for racing,

no time lost in silly lacing.

They will not pinch or raise a blister

or get passed down to Baby Sister.

Perfect fit, very neat,

made especially for the heat—

your very own skinny-boned, wiggly-toed

FEET.